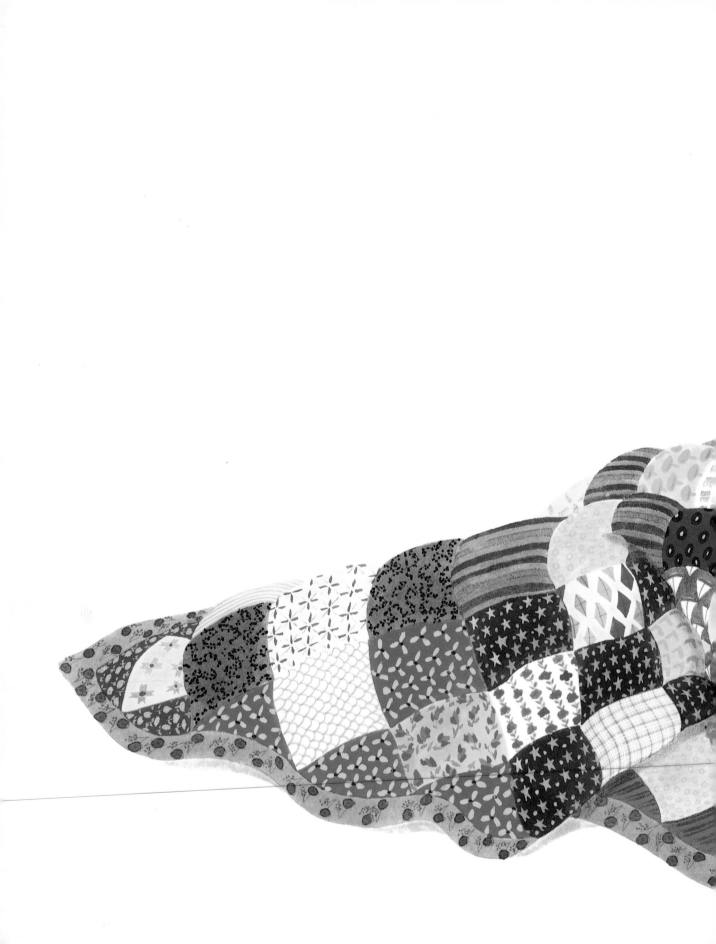

Copyright © 1984 by Ann Jonas
All rights reserved. No part of this
book may be reproduced or utilized
in any form or by any means, elec-
tronic or mechanical, including pho-
tocopying, recording or by any infor-
mation storage and retrieval system,
without permission in writing from the
Publisher, Greenwillow Books,
an imprint of HarperCollins Publishers,
10 East 53rd Street,
New York, NY 10022.
Manufactured in China by South China
Printing Company Ltd.
First Edition
11 12 13 SCP 10
Library of Congress Cataloging
in Publication Data
Jonas, Ann. The quilt.
Summary: A child's new patch-
work quilt recalls old memories and
provides new adventures at bedtime.
[1. Quilts—Fiction.
2. Bedtime—Fiction] I. Title.
PZ7.J664Qi 1984   [E]   83-25385
ISBN 0-688-03825-5
ISBN 0-688-03826-3 (lib. bdg.)

The Quilt
Ann Jonas

Greenwillow Books/New York

I have a new quilt.

It's to go on my
new grown-up bed.

My mother and father
made it for me. They used
some of my old things.
Here are my first curtains
and my crib sheet. Sally
is lying on my baby pajamas.

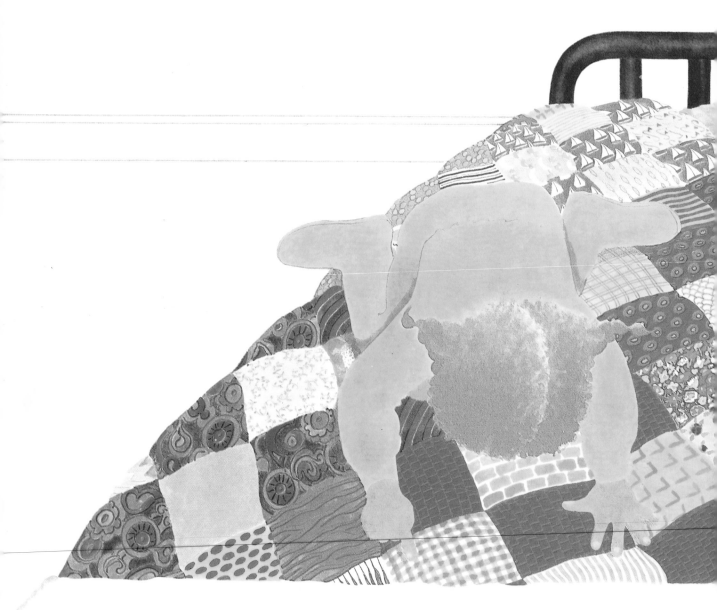

That's the shirt I wore on
my second birthday.
This piece is from my
favorite pants. They got
too small. The cloth my
mother used to make Sally
is here somewhere.
I can't find it now.

I know I won't be able
to go to sleep tonight.

It almost looks
like a little town....

I can't find Sally!

Maybe she's here.
Sally!

She wouldn't like it here.
Sally!

What if someone
took her home?
Sally!

If she hid here,
I'd never find her.
Sally!

What a scary tunnel!
I'll run through fast.
Sally! Sally! Sally!
Sally! Sally! Sally!

She wouldn't be here.
She doesn't like water.
Sally!

I see her!

Good
morning,
Sally.